Sex in the Strangest Places!

A Little about the Author:

Lakyshia L. (Shelton) Hubert was born in Pahokee
Florida, raised in Clewiston Florida. She's the
youngest of seven siblings and a host of stepsisters.
Oldest sister Renee Shelton, Tachia Shelton,
Yolanda Coulson, Teresa Burnett, Cecilia Williams
and Lorenzo Shelton Jr. her loving mother Mary
(Burnett) Shelton and Lorenzo Shelton Sr has
blessed them with so much knowledge and wisdom,
until they didn't know they was raising a young
author. Lakyshia (better known as Keke) brother
was filled with talent such as: Singing, Dancing,
writing poetry, writing music, and Drawing. Lakyshia
felt like she was left with nothing, until one day she
read all the things she kept hidden and realized that
she also can write poetry. The problem was she
could only write them when she was sad and hurt.
Then she ended up going away for a while that's
when one day just began writing and she ended up
with this book. It may have taken her sometime, but

2

she would like for all of you to know it was worth the wait, when you rush to do things and try to outdo someone you will never make it far because, writing should be from your heart and should be written with care, not rushed through. So, with that being said please enjoy this book, and again the author would like to thank each and every one who took time out to purchase and read this novel.

Thanks in advance

Mrs.Hubert

Table of Contents

4

Prologue

Please enjoy the everlasting lust of sex from one mind to another, this book is about things learned over the years from talking to different couples, straight, gay's, bisexual, and single people, etc. Please understand that this book is for adults only and things do get very very tempting. So, if you're a woman that's curious, a couple who's looking to spice up your sex life or someone with a wild imagination then this is the book for you.

The Beginning

Shondra and her friends are going to a party; they get dressed up and head out the door. As they arrive Shondra spots Keisha and Peaches, Carmen parks the car and they jump out and begin to conversate. Peaches say let's go inside the party is jumping and the drinks are going around. The ladies enter the party and are escorted to the drinks; they see strippers on the pole upside down. "Wow says the ladies "come on let's find us something to get into. The women begin to dance with random men laughing and grinding. The DJ say it's getting pretty heated in here let me play some to set the mood. That's when (Beyoncé-dance for you) begin to play. Ladies grabbing their partner/mate and you can tell that sex is in the air. The DJ playing all these love making songs, the guy grabs Shondra and lead her to the deck of the pool. He lays her on a blanket and begins to massage her body with his strong hands. Shondra butt cheeks are spread and next thing she know this man sticks his tongue in her butt hole. Shondra never experienced nothing like this before, he has two fingers caressing her clitoris and it's getting wetter and wetter. Carmen is inside the bathroom with these two random men who she was dancing with all night. One of them is sitting on the edge of the tub and Carmen is bent over giving him head as the other one is fucking her fat, wet, juicy, throbbing vagina. The other one continues to fuck her butt, and then they switch back and forth, from getting head, anal, freaking each other etc. Meanwhile Peaches lies on the couch spreads her legs and slide one finger into her vagina, then another. The party continues and the DJ spots Peaches fondling herself, so he heads over with his penis erupted. He grabs her and shoves his penis inside her mouth and she swallow his manhood. She licks his balls and the crack of his ass; she then takes her finger and play around his butt, while sucking his penis. His toes began to curl, and his eyes roll in the back of his head. Then he sits on the couch and tell Peaches to ride his cock, she gets on top with her pussy already dripping wet and he's nibbling on her ear, neck and suckling her nipples as she goes up and down. There's then Keisha whom is inside the kitchen on the counter, with pineapples all over her and three girls sucking them off. One girl inserts a twizzler inside Keisha and eats it back out, with her mouth. The ladies are moaning and groaning, taking turns fucking each other with the sex toys. Everyone is enjoying themselves, its ass smacking and cock sucking all around. Shondra is at the pool enjoying every moment of this man who has her up on his shoulders eating her butt and vagina. Carmen is wrapped up in the bathroom with these two men who have her in every which way possible. Keisha is with the women, but Peaches is pissed, she heads into the kitchen and interrupt Keisha. They began to talk and that's when Peaches tell her what happened. They both start laughing by the end of the conversation, and head to the bedroom. Now the women are chatting, when Peaches turn the TV on porn (ass for days was the name) the women sit and watch these as all these sexy women are bending over and showing their fat vagina's. The camera man says damn girl, as one of them lay on her back and shows her vagina off. So, Peaches and Keisha began to kiss each other, they are rubbing bodies together; they are squeezing each other butts. Keisha licks Peaches nipples, they put on the strap and now it's time for fucking. The women are enjoying each other not realizing the sun has risen. Someone is knocking at the door; calling their name saying would y'all hurry up. Shondra screams at them as she walks out the door. Carmen hits the door one more time and Keisha says ok we are coming out. Back in the car the ladies began to tell stories on how the events took place and what had happened in the days before last night.

CHAPTER ONE: show me

Shondra a mother of two boys is struggling to make it on a daily basis. She's scared to love because of the hurt and pain she been through so many times. Then one day Shondra bumps into this guy whom she has known awhile, every time they we're around each other she gets nervous. She walks up and says hello Jamie (the whole time thinking damn this one fine caramel, tall 6'00, medium built, sexy brown eye man) Jamie says hello Shondra I've been meaning to talk with you, "just hear me out ok!" I think you're very beautiful and I would like to date you. Two weeks later while chilling with him on the park, Shondra turn to him and says daddy rub my stomach, touch me anyway you like because as of tonight this body belongs to you. Jamie caresses her body gently then he kisses her on the neck softly.

Oohh "baby she screams as he slowly kisses and caresses her vagina with his tongue. Shondra begin to moan more, and more as Jamie stroke her pussy with his tongue speeding up little by little. She tries to run, but he grasps her legs and holds her into that position. She feels her body start to melt while he steady pleasuring her, Jamie slides one finger into her ass then two. They switch positions, so now Shondra is on top of Jamie as he slowly enters his 12inch cock inside her throbbing vagina. She ridding as Jamie pulls her head back she screams his name. "Jamie Jamie "he kisses her, whisper and nibble on her ear. Jamie pulls out as she shakes, vagina soak and wet he nuts on her stomach. Shondra realize the time and jumps up to run home. Now back home in the shower she's thinking about Jamie and what fun they had. After she done she goes into her room saying should I call him and let him know I enjoyed myself? When suddenly there's a knock at her window. Shondra looks up to see Jamie, she lets him inside. He says baby I just couldn't stop thinking of you, he kisses her lips gently and lay Shondra on the bed. Jamie is working his way down her body suckling on her nipples. Jamie kisses Shondra on the belly. She shivers as he began to slowly enter his tongue into her sweet vagina, that's throbbing to have him. He's hitting all the right spots it's hard for Shondra not to scream and shout. He slides one finger in her pussy, and then slowly slides one more while still licking on, sucking on, the little man in the boat, (spur tongue). Shondra lay Jamie down on the bed and begin to suck his nice lone 12inch dick. She's licking on his balls, placing both of them in her mouth. Shondra slowly grabs his dick stroking it up and down with her hands, while at the same time she's still sucking it and playing with his balls. Jamie eyes start to roll in the back of his head and toes began to curl. Now they're doing the 69 position when the window pops open. Paul and Peaches come in, now the candles are lit, and the music starts to play slowly and softly. (Love faces by: Trey Songs) Peaches and Paul (two friends of Jamie and Shondra) join them in bed. Peaches (5'5, medium woman build, ass like whoa, breast are so big and pretty, her lips so sexy and soft) start to kiss Shondra vagina also caressing her ass with her tongue, While Jamie slips a finger inside peaches pussy. Paul is just sitting back looking at peaches and Shondra. Paul has (a nice tall, dark skinned and thick man), corn rolls in his head and his eyes are light brown) playing with his 10inch dick. now Jamie and Paul is sitting side by side on the bed, then Shondra and peaches takes turns sucking both men dicks. Shondra gets up and lay Peaches down on the bed and then starts kissing her nipples. Paul sticks his dick in Peaches mouth and Jamie does the same. So, Peaches is sucking both their dicks while Shondra is kissing Peaches clitoris. Jamie has a finger inside Shondra wet vagina and Paul has a finger inside Shondra ass. Jamie grabs Shondra and

13

begin to fuck her in the doggy style position meanwhile Peaches is ridding Paul. The sound of love making is in the air. Peaches and Shondra lies side by side as Paul and Jamie takes turns fucking both of them. They are kissing and touching each other, Jamie puts Shondra on top as Paul is still fucking peaches when suddenly she couldn't stop it from coming. She grasps, and Jamie grabs her waist grinding his big dick further inside of her vagina then they both came. Paul got peaches legs in the air you can hear them grunt and groan as they explode in ecstasy. Now it's time for them to go, and Shondra have never felt so pleased in her life. She runs to take a shower then she dots some notes in her journal, and fast asleep she goes dreaming of everything that happened earlier that night.

CHAPTER TWO: YOUR LUST

Carmen was the school most popular girl. All the boys loved when she just came their way, but little did they know Carmen was a sneaky freak. One day Carmen met Paul, soon as they laid eyes on each other it was an instant connection. Paul walked up to Carmen (5'7, 160lbs, Puerto Rican and black, long black curly hair, and hazel eyes) he said hello I'm Paul and I was wondering if I could get to know you? They then exchanged numbers and went on their separate way, and later that evening Paul called Carmen and they talked. Carmen wanted to know if Peaches was his girlfriend! Paul says no we are just friends who love to explore things and have fun sex with each other. She replies ok that's fine, so Paul says come meet me down on the park beside the big tree, where you can see the sun setting on the horizon. Carmen arrives at the park and Paul is waiting for her with a blanket laid out and two wine glasses along with a picnic basket. He grabs Carmen and softly kisses her cheek, they sit down, and Paul takes the food out and says I've made something for you. He then begins to feed Carmen some grilled T-bone steak, scalloped potatoes, and dinner rolls. She's also feeding him with her finger, so he is kissing all over her hands. He then fixes then a glass of wine and feed her sum mixed fruit. Now they lay down cuddling when Paul whispers in her ear, "I want to play in your pussy till you want me to stop. He's kissing her neck, nibbling at her ear, and also pushing is masculine hard dick up against her ass. Paul say's Carmen I want to lick your pussy ill suck it, caress it, I need you and want to feel your beautiful soft body right against mine. Carmen looks Paul in the eyes, smiles and says yes Paul you can play with me, inside me, and all over me. I'll be the desert she says as she sprays whip cream and fruit all over her body. I want to feel your tongue run down my body bay, from front to back. Carmen put chocolate covered strawberries around her nipples. Paul stands up to take his pants off and Carmen could see his nature rising. Paul eats the whipped cream and strawberries off her. He makes a trail down her stomach to her vagina; it's pretty pink and fat. He slowly slides his tongue in Carmen pussy feeling it getting wetter and wetter. Paul rotates his tongue around Carmen spur tongue licking it like its melting ice cream, that's he trying to catch before it melts. Paul asks how many licks it takes to get to the center. Carmen says let do the 69ner position I'll please you while you're pleasing me. Now it's time for Carmen to climb on top of that dick. O yes that juicy 10 1/2-inch dick is all the way inside her; Carmen riding that dick like it's a rollercoaster. Paul says lay down let me see what you're really about, so Carmen then lay flat on her belly and slide his dick deeply inside her ass. He says are you sure you ready for this ride lil mama. Yes, daddy she replies! He starts to fuck that ass with a deep long thrust. Carmen's moaning very loudly as the sun setting reflects off their body. He goes left to right, very hard then slowing it down. She gets on top of Paul with her ass towards his face and holding his legs while slow winding on his dick as he spanks her ass. Soon as Carmen begins to catch her orgasm Paul pulls her off the dick. He then turns her around and start fucking her from the back, long stroke, short stroke, fast, hard, slow, and gentle. Now Carmen's shaking because he is hitting all the right spots. Paul now put Carmen ass in the buck. Ooooohhhh baby it feels so good to me, yes fuck me harder and harder baby. Paul kisses her while he's lifting her body up from the ground. He then makes her stand up and bend over on the tree as he's pounding that nice thick dick deep inside her wet vagina. Carmen is cumin as he steady fucking her and he says get on your knees I'm about to masturbate, open your mouth and stick your tongue out, lick on the head of this dick, says Paul as "he pushes his dick deep down Carmen throat while she plays with his nut sack. He pulls her hair back and say yes suck daddy dick just like that! Spit on this dick and suck that shit awww yes, he grunts baby that's what I'm talking about right there you're a freak. Carmen swallows Paul dick and bring it back out with no problem. He grabs her head and says o shit I'm cumin is you ready for me. She opens her mouth wide as he cum inside her mouth. They lay down to cuddle when suddenly his phone rings. They clean up kiss and go their separate ways. Carmen walks inside the house and make a bath then there is a ring at the door. Carmen grabs a towel and run-down stairs to open the door. Paul, she says "what are you doing here? Paul grabs her kisses her and says I had to come back for one last kiss. She began to blush as she closes the door and go return to her bath.

CHAPTER THREE: FAVORITE SPOT

Shondra tells peaches to ride with her to the doctor office because she's feeling a little sick. so, they pull up and go sign in, while being seated inside the room to wait for the doctor peaches says girl it's some lingerie on the chair. Shondra replies girl this going to be the best doctor visit we've been to in a longtime. Put it on and wrap the robe around you. (While Peaches is changing, and Shondra is thinking yes, I've been waiting for this moment) the doctor walks in and says Ms. Shondra I understand you are feeling woozy, and your vision was blurry. yes, she replies" he say well I'm Doctor Ken and I'll be at your service. Just give me a minute and I'll be right back. When the door closes Peaches says damn girl Dr. Ken is so fine. (He's short, cocky built, with light brown eyes) where did you find his ask Peaches.

The doctor return to the room and say Shondra I didn't know you had a friend with you. So, they introduce themselves and Shondra sits down in the chair and says can you check my temperature doctor. He spreads her legs and says tell me where are you feeling hot, as he pulls out his dick. Peaches start to stroke his dick as Shondra lick the head of his pelvis. He's grabbing both Shondra and Peaches hair. Pussy check time says the doctor, so the women lay on top of each other! Dr. Ken pulls the chair over and says my, what do we have here?! He starts by sticking one finger inside Peaches vagina, and then with the other hand he slides a finger into Shondra pussy. Peaches is squeezing on Shondra breast as the doc softly kiss and tongue fuck they clitoris one at a time. Shondra gets up and let doc lay down on the bed, as peaches is sucking his dick. He pulls her head to guide her mouth further on his dick. Shondra is on her knees caressing peaches clit with two fingers while softly nibbling on her ass cheek. They're moaning, now switch and Peaches slides her tongue inside Shondra ass while fingering her vagina. Then she switches and sticks two fingers in Shondra ass and makes Shondra squat down on top of her face, so she can ride the tongue. All the while Shondra is sucking, Doctor Ken's balls and jacking his dick, and then she switches and goes on that dick. He calls for Peaches to come join Shondra... Now they both taking turns sucking, licking and kissing all over Doctor Ken dick and balls, now Shondra gets on top and go to riding the doctor's dick. Peaches is standing behind Shondra still sucking on doc's balls... He grabs Shondra around her hips and tells her to get up because he doesn't want to nut yet. So, he now has Shondra and Peaches bent over the bed, he slowly slides his cock into Peaches vagina at the same time entering a finger into Shondra ass and pussy. The girls are kissing and moaning as Doctor Ken switches from one to another, then just as the women climax he tells both of them to get on their knees and he cum in both of their faces... Now after they're done cleaning up the doctor steps out and returns... When he returns he had a smile on his face as he tells them the pussy passed the test and he would like to see them in two weeks... But as they walked out to leave he says I wrote down my address I'm going to need y'all to come to my house later tonight at eight o'clock... The ladies reply is there a problem doc... He smiled and said why yes there is one more exam I need to perform on y'all to see if y'all will pass... Shondra and Peaches replies ok doctor we will be there....

Chapter Four: Where's My G-spot

Jamie wakes up to a smell which has his mouth watering and his stomach growling... He walks and turns the shower on and washes his face, and then he jumps inside the shower... Not knowing Shondra done been up for about two hours preparing his breakfast. Shondra lays his clothes, boxers, socks and shoes out and run back down stairs to get his food. Now Jamie is out the shower drying off when he notices the shoes and clothes on the bed... He smiled and walks out the bathroom that's when he sees his food; Jamie says damn baby done threw down! He has pork chops, eggs, grits and toasted bread with jelly on it, along with that some coffee and orange juice... He eats then gets dressed walks down stairs and see two unfamiliar faces in the kitchen with Shondra, Jamie says good morning, gives her a kiss... Shondra says baby I want you to introduce you to Keisha (which she is about 5'4 160lbs phatt ass and big tits, she Cuban and Puerto Rican with a little black) and Miguel (she is 5'8 200lbs solid muscle Mexican and Jamaican) Keisha says hello Jamie! Shondra and I were just talking about a G-spots and I realized she is where I once was until I started asking around and my cousin told me about this website called Askman.com... Keisha goes on to tell them everything she learned. Dr. Ernst Graf Enberg discovered the G-spot in 1950, and the actual Ares is about the size of a quarter but feels rougher then the surrounding tissue Shondra and Jamie is like damn Keisha you and Miguel is some freaks.... They all laughed, and Miguel tells them oh there's is more. This doctor explained thoroughly and now we are going to share this information with y'all. Keisha tells Shondra in order for your man to locate and master the G-spot; he has to face you while you're lying on your back... (Shondra and Jamie do just what Keisha and Miguel is showing them) now insert your index or middle finger into her vagina as far as it will easily go... A lot of men thought the clitoris was considered the only trigger for the female orgasm, even finding the female's clitoris turned out to be a daunting task for many men, and things didn't get easier in the 1950's when Dr. Ernst Graf Enberg found, and even more mysterious female pleasure spot hidden within the vagina. Keisha said, "Y'all stay with me because we learned a lot from this article." This area became popular by sexologist in the 80's as the G-spot. The stimulation of the G-spot produces a very powerful kind of orgasm in some women... it even produces females ejaculation, colloquially known as squirting now for both of these reasons, finding stimulating and discovering how to master the women G-spot has become for both men and women, the holy grail of female pleasuring... Keisha goes on to tell them that as she read further into this article it also said the G-spot is the bean-shaped tissue of the par-urethral gland which is analogous to the male prostate. The actual area is only about the size of a quarter, but it feels rougher to touch then the surrounding tissue, because the G-spot is composed of erectile tissue, it swells up when blood rushes to it, especially if you learn how to master the G-spot effectively. Now it's located about two inches back from the vaginal opening inside the front vaginal wall. The front wall is the wall of the vagina on the same side as her belly button. (Keisha said the best part last but not least), the best way to find the G-spot, first of all the G-spot is easiest to locate when the woman is sexually aroused, so don't stint on your foreplay first. (Now since you are already laying on your back with the men facing us, with one index finger inserted as far as it will easily go), next he has to crook his finger up towards himself in a come hither motion, sliding his fingertip along the top of the vagina until he find an area that is rougher than the rest of that vaginal wall. This rough or slightly ridged area is the G-spot and touching it will often cause the woman to react with surprise or pleasure. So, Jamie does just what he was told, and he realized just when he found it because Shondra began to quiver and moan. Jamie motions to Keisha and Miguel for them to join, the lights are dim, and the music is playing softly. Keisha kisses on Shondra as Miguel and Jamie is taking turns eating both women vagina. Shondra switches up and begin sucking both Jamie and Miguel rock hard cocks. Miguel lays Shondra down and goes directly to her G-spot; while Jamie has a little trouble locating Keisha's, but they are helping each other learn. Jamie has Keisha up with her back against the wall fucking her slowly and passionately. She's biting his neck and digging her nails into his back. Miguel has Shondra in the doggy style, spanking her ass and pulling her hair. Both ladies begin to moan loudly as they are now climaxing with pleasure; the men have both ladies suckling their penis until they ejaculate all in the ladies' mouth. After cleaning up Miguel and Keisha gives Jamie and Shondra hugs, then say's just remember what I told y'all about the G-spot and trust me you will master it.

Chapter Five: Between My Legs

Shondra end up being arrested for unpaid parking tickets, now she's sitting behind bars wondering if any of her friends going to come to visit her. Then she hears her name being called on the loud speaker: get dressed Ms. Shondra you're headed down to cell block 69! Shondra replies do I need to pack my things? Yes, ma'am you do because you're being held 48hours for some test. The officer will be in shortly for you. The officer arrives and says I'm CEO Carmen, I'm going to need you to place your hands on the wall. She then begins to slowly rub her hands down Shondra legs and up again. She began to get hot all over, sorry officer it's been awhile since I've been touched that way! Just don't let it happen again the officer replies in this familiar tone... open cell block 69, Shondra heard moaning screaming, and her heart beginning to race. Why am I here? This is your cell replied Carmen as she walks away... Now a lady name Keisha walks in and says "Please stand and face the wall.... Shondra does as she is told, that's when she hear this voice telling her to drop her shirt that when she caught the voice and said Peaches what are you doing here?... We here to surprise you, Carmen, Keisha and I after Shondra is undressed, Carmen enters the room holding a platter with four wine glasses and fruits with whip cream on top. She then stepped back out and returned with sex oil, handcuffs, chocolate covered panties, etc. They rubbed hot oil on each other gave massages, then Peaches slides her finger into Keisha Vagina, Carmen starts to kiss Shondra on her breast then she works her way down in between her legs caressing her pussy with her tongue. Now cell block 69 is starting to heat up. Just as the ladies are switching positions a bag is left by the door there is two double headed 10-inch dildos inside. The ladies take sips from the wine and put whip cream and pineapples on the dildo and sucks it off. Shondra and Carmen enter the dildo into their pussy... Peaches insert the end of the second dildo into her ass and Keisha does also. Now there's moaning and ass slapping, Shondra reaches into the basket and takes out her strap on. She tells Keisha to bend over then Shondra begin to slowly fuck her in the ass. Peaches and Carmen is doing the 69ner... sex in the air! Carmen takes Shondra strap and slides it into Keisha pussy, as Carmen and Shondra are fingering each other. Keisha is moaning loudly as Peaches pounds harder and harder while she grabs by the waist and goes deeper and deeper. Keisha is shaking and say's here I cum! Carmen is using the strap on penis on Shondra, Carmen says let me see how you ride that dick! So Shondra is on top and Peaches is sucking her breast. Keisha is licking peaches vagina while fingering herself. that's when there's a knock at the door and it appear to be this fine, short, dark buff man who happen to have a voice that make a woman just want to take her clothes off right there and then. His name was Travis; it also was another tall kind of slim Carmel brother with a sexy New York accent named Kevin! Travis walks inside the room and says ladies can my home boy and I join y'all? The ladies reply sure why not! The men get undressed and Travis walks towards Shondra and say what can you do with these 12 inches? Shondra responds why you don't come over here with me and my friend K to find out. The whole while Kevin had done joined Peaches and Carmen with his huge 10inch cock. Carmen began to suck Kevin penis while he's eating peaches vagina. He slowly enters a finger into peaches ass while he's licking her clitoris. Shondra is playing with Carmen pussy, as Travis began to enter his penis into Shondra vagina, she moans softly. K is having her pussy ate by both Kevin and Peaches, as they began to switch positions. Kevin says ladies lay on top one of one another in sets of twos'! the ladies comply (cell block 69 is heating up) then Kevin is fucking one then the other, as Travis is fucking Carmen and kissing on Shondra breast. Shondra is riding Travis face and peaches is riding his dick all while tongue kissing each other, Carmen is eating K pussy while Kevin is fucking her hard from the back in doggy style... There's moaning, kissing, licking and sex everywhere... The ladies begin to scream and shake as their body collapse in ecstasy. At this point everyone is having orgasm. The room gets quiet as everyone is coming down off of an emotional ecstasy high, and then they all fall asleep.

Chapter six: Kit-Kat Island

*ATTETION PLEASE READ IMPORTANT
INFORMATION YOU SHOULD KNOW. *

Welcome to an island like no other an explicit
retreat. During your stay there are three important
things you must know, and you must aware of while
on this erotic island vacation:

(The first thing that you should know) We strongly
suggest that you have a partner, but it is not
required you will see a lot of erotic activities the will
have your hormones jumping out of body.

(The second thing that need to know) If you're a
senior and you're going to complain THIS IS NOT
THE PLACE FOR YOU. This island is for the young,
wild, freaky, and sexy people will be walking around
nude. (WARNING THERE WILL BE LOTS OF

MOANING, GROANING, SCREAMING, MAYBE EVEN HOLLERING ON THIS EROTIC ISLAND KNOW AS KIT-KAT ISLAND)

(The final thing you should know) Please bring your own sexual items such as oil toys straps whatever gets you hot and tempted. This is because some of the MEN and or WOMEN might not be all you expected them to be, WOMEN also bring your best skimpiest noticeable outfits. This will enhance your vacation to one will never ever forget. Absolutely no animals allowed just you and your goodies. Now we hope that you enjoy Kit-Kat Island the most erotic island vacation in the world.

P.S. If there are any questions comments and or problems contact management at the front desk of the resort and will be happy to assist you.

THANK YOU,

KIT-KAT ISLAND MANAGMENT

(The phone call)

Carmen: hello Peaches

Peaches: yea girl how are you doing

Carmen: I'm good, But Keisha asked me to call you; and see if you and Shondra are going to be here today!

Peaches: hold on for one-minute girl (Shondra will you bring your behind on here)! Carmen girl we are at the airport, and Shondra is walking slowly as if we got a lot of time on our side. (LOL) But tell Keisha we're supposed to arrive around 4:30pm it is 10:15am now.

Carmen: ok I'll let her know, because girl ooohhh girl y'all don't know what y'all missing right now. It is some sexy ass men out here.

Peaches: laughs and says girl you got issues. I'll call you when we make our last switch over because after that I'll be calling to say we're there.

Carmen: ok baby y'all be careful.

Peaches: ok girl

(PHONES HANG UP)

(BACK AT THE ROOM)

Carmen takes a shower at the spot they reserved overlooking the beautiful wave and the breath-taking beach view. It's a huge shower so big 6 people could fit inside. So, Carmen steps in the shower the light are dim trey songs (The neighbors know my name) playing. Carmen never sipped Don Perion before but there was a fresh bottle of the French smooth white champagne sitting chilled. She sips the song change to R-Kelly bump and grind as she washed her body she reaches in her bag and pull out her big black 9in dildo!!!!!! Then turns it on slow.......She strokes it in and out of her already dipping wet pussy......She moans oh my god yes as she fucks herself while licking her big round tits. She keeps fucking herself until she cum. Carmen finishes her shower than she does her hair and puts on her little (pink) see through boy shorts and a half top with no (bra) she lotions up and put on her pink pumps and goes to find Keisha.

Carmen says as she walks out of the room let me call Keisha.

(THE PHONE IS RINGING)

Keisha: Hello Hello

Carmen: Where you at girl? We have to meet Peaches and Shondra at the airport.

Keisha: Ok I'm going to meet you at the bar.

(THE PHONE CALL ENDS)

Meanwhile Peaches and Shondra step off the plane and say wow it looks nice out here.

(Peaches pick up her phone and calls Carmen.)

Peaches: Hello girl we're here

Carmen: We are standing at the front of the airport waiting.

Peaches: ok

They all meet up and head back to the resort and chat and laugh for a while. Then Peaches and Shondra shower up and get dress and head to check out the island.

While they stroll about the island they were amazed at what they were seeing, couples stroking each other up and whipping one another. It was pussy, ass, and dick slinging all over the place all shapes and sizes!

The girl's make their way upstairs to the freak fest party and take a seat the bar and order some drinks. While sitting there drinking their drinks a nice dark skinned medium built fella walks up and approach Carmen and says hi beautiful would you like to join me. She said sure and got up and walks away with him. Meanwhile Keisha and Shondra are both enjoying the Jacuzzi....Peaches leaves and joins Carmen. This nice looking fine man leans back and watch as Peaches and Carmen are kissing, touching, and rubbing all over each other. Peaches is now tickling Carmen clitoris with her tongue, and Carmen slides her index finger inside Peaches ass. Now Carmen is making eyes contact with this handsome God of a man whom she nicknames (Fresh Black) so he can see as she inserts her tongue deep inside of Peaches pretty pink (spur tongue). Finally, Fresh Black stands up and moves swiftly towards the bed. He then picked Carmen up in the air with her back against the wall and legs wrapped around his head. Peaches, unzips Blacks pants and begins to suck on his dick. Carmen is enjoying herself with Peaches and Fresh Black in every way imaginable.

(KEISHA and SHONDRA)

Back over at the Jacuzzi the other girl relaxing when the waitress walks up with drinks and says the gentlemen across by the bar sent these drink and requests that y'all join them. Shondra and Keisha are like damn men treat you like that here. Everyone has a laugh as the girl get up to go meet the men. Jerry and Gary, was their names, they look like some Greek Gods with chocolate skin complexion. They had this African accent which made the girls more excited. They have a dance and drink the twins are grinding and slow winding slinging their dicks that look like they weigh 1000 pounds like they know how to use them. Keisha and Jerry walk away into the men's room inside of a stall where Jerry sticks his whole hand up into her already wet, dripping, and throbbing pussy. He pops out her big round juicy breast and starts slowly kissing and sucking them if they were a baby's bottle. He then bends Keisha over and places his thick two-ton penis inside her already soaked vagina........ He pulls her by the hair and slaps her on the ass Keisha can't believe what is happening to her at this moment, but hell it feels damn good. She gets weak at the knees and she begin to Trimble as she says yes Jerry fuck this pussy.

Shondra and Gary finally realizing they are by themselves try to figure out what are they going to do now. Gary grabs Shondra's hand and says let's take walk. They began walking toward the beach then Gary says let's stop right here this seems like a perfect place for us. They sit, talk, and laugh as they share funny stories... Shondra says my backs a little stiff, would you massage it for me? Gary says of course and un-strap her bra, then takes his baby soft hand and starts to rub her back, up and down slowly, but very softly. He now gets a little firmer as he rubs her up and down just like she likes it to be done. Shondra takes her shorts off and Gary massages her ass, Shondra feels her hormone jumping she is getting horny. She then turns and pulls Gary closer as he pulls back her head and starts kissing her neck. They kiss then pull out his 10 1/2-inch dick and shows Shondra. She quickly grabs it with her mouth and as soon as she makes about four to five strokes Gary lays down on his back and Shondra gets on tops and enjoys the ride. The waves crushing on their sides as she says yes Gary yes yes feels so good fuck, Gary reply ride this dick girl you're a big girl baby yes. The sun now begins to roll in and all the girls are meeting back up to the room with smiles... Shondra is inside the shower Keisha says damn she must have put on him pointing at the shower.

(The door squeaks) Gary says hello baby with an accent Shondra says, what are you doing here? He replies I just couldn't let you slip away without seeing you one more time. Shondra smiles and kisses him passionately.

Everyone eats laugh, take pictures, and walk around and enjoy the scenery one more time before they have to catch their fight.

After they say their last good-bye the women load up onto the plane with other passengers, but now the spot light on Shondra because everyone is wondering about Gary and she leaves it that way.

Chapter Seven: Sex in a Light House

Shondra, Keisha, Peaches, and Carmen gather all the men together (Paul, Dr. Ken, Jamie, And Travis) and said let's go have sex in a light house, then play truth or dare. Everyone is like Shondra what are you talking about? So Shondra say's sit down and let me tell y'all a story. Everyone then pulls a chair to form a circle, so Shondra can see them and they can see her.

Shondra starts by telling them this poem her brother wrote for her and a friend before they went and had sex in a light house!

Sex in a Light House

You're feeling hot and you're lit up inside looking for that special someone. Then I come along, we get to know each other better. One day I say we're here! We go inside the light house to talk and have some fun. It goes from 9 to 10:30 pretty quickly. We look in each other eyes and our lips begin to touch. I lick your navel, kissing my way down suckling your spur tongue as if it was a baby bottle. I then turn you over and put my 10 1/2-inch cock inside your tight vagina, stroke, stroke, stroke you say yes daddy fuck me. Harder, harder o yes it feels so good to me. We masturbate, and you lay there happy and full of life. That's when I turn to you and say how you feel about just having sex in a light house?

Keisha say's: ok my turn, Sex in a Light House

As the sun begins to set in the horizon, I look upon your face and say while you're here on the beach, let's check out the light house. As we enter the stairs crack and the door creaks, you grab my hand and pull me close. We walk further up the stairs after lighting candles. Then as we reached the top, you spread the cover on the floor and lay me on my back, spread my legs, and rip my underwear off.

You're dripping oil down my legs and softly caressing them. You're kissing my navel and squeezing my nipples. I can feel my vagina getting soak and wet, throbbing for affection. Your body is so masculine and solid on top of mine, as you begin to insert your giant cock slowly into my vagina. I grasp every time you stroke o so deeply in and out. Yes, daddy I yell over and over again. There's ass slapping, moaning and groaning all in the air. Our bodies began to shake as we done had sex in a light house.

Peaches: Sex in a Light House

The rain drips against the window pane. The silence fills the air and there you we're just as fine as could be. The music softly blazes in the background and I can feel the tension roaming in the air. The chemistry between you and I cannot be retained, I slowly begin to dance for you, winding my ass up against you. I can feel your nature rising as I slowly unwind. I lay you against the stair way as the light shine from the light house. I climb on top of you and begin to ride as you smack my ass then grunt so loudly. You say baby I want it another way, so bend over and assume the position. You are now fucking me from the back as I push and throw this hot, wet pussy back. You're pulling my hair as I say daddy give ne more and more. We change positions once again because I think someone is headed for the door. Precious pieces o so sweet, now that's a big meat to treat, stroking me slow then hard and fast. Daddy that's the way I make it last, sex in a light house you shall see because now it's you inside of me. He then snatches me up in the air you'd thought he was spider man, up against the wall he has me with my legs over his shoulder making me scream. Now this is my kind of fantasy, sex in a light house this will be for as long as you are here with me.

Carmen: Sex in a Light House

Here with me, you wake to smell bacon and eggs. You head in the bathroom to wash your face and ask is this just a dream. I say baby are you ok, for this is just the beginning of our day. What do you say; today you will see just how much you mean to me. So, come here let me be your queen, there's nothing you will need. Sex in a light house will be fun you see, now that your body is next to me. I spit on your cock while you're standing in front of me, then I began sucking your steadily rising hard dick. You then push your dick so deep in my throat I thought I was going to choke and slob all down your balls. Slurp slurp is all you hear as I'm licking you from front to rear. Your eyes roll in the back of your head, you scream and shout out my name. Sex in a light house since you are here with me; now bend over as I slide my finger in & out your ass! I place some Vaseline all over your erupted penis, then spreading my ass cheeks and placing it in my ass hole so deeply. I wonder what he will do to me! I like it rough and fast, let me throw it back while you in fucking me roughly inside my ass. Sex in a light house, now let's see how freaky you're willing to be with me?!

Everyone then looks at each other and says damn I'm horny; now let's go check out Sex in a light house. We're pulling up to the light house and we all get out quickly. Once inside, we start drinking and toasting. Keisha plays some music softly as everyone is chatting, dancing, and singing! That's when Shondra pulls out her toy and spread her legs then slid it inside! Carmen, Keisha, Peaches, Dr. Ken, Paul, Travis, and Jamie instantly remove their clothing. Travis grabs peaches and head to the other side of the light house. He spreads her legs and begins to kiss her clit with his tongue, and he made her cum quickly, legs shaking and trembling, as weak as can be. Jamie and Keisha head to the shower in the lighthouse, and they turn it on. Jamie quickly slides his penis inside Keisha vagina, pounding harder with each and every stroke. Meanwhile Dr. Ken is on the chair with Carmen ass spread wide in his face, tonguing her ass and finger fucking her vagina. Aaww shit yes is all you hear around the light house. Paul grabs Shondra and throw the toy out the way, he say's Sex in a light house is what you're going to get today. Get on your knees and back that ass up towards me. He's holding her waist, stroking nice and slowly as can be. Now everyone is taking turns with one another, Sex in a light house is what you will receive if you think you can handle this. Here are all of us, but especially about you being with me. After finishing the sex, we sit back and laugh telling one another what a good time we had, also marking the date down on the calendar for our next date of Sex in a light house.

Thanks for taking time out to support and read my book, because with my fans and readers, we all have a chance. Now please take your time out to read the sequel, Thanks again and please be on the lookout for more coming soon.

The author,

Mrs. Lakyshia L (Shelton) Hubert

Sequel: Sex in the Strangest Places Part Two

When You Think No One Is Watching!

Tiana calls her friend Mya and says: girl I found this book my mama ordered, it's called Sex in the strangest places!

Mya: really girl your mama going to be looking for that book.

Tiana replies: I heard my mama tell her friends that it was really juicy and whenever she sees me standing there she yells at me, go to your room or outside, you are too young to be listening to our conversation. I say to myself wow I'm 17 now.

Mya says: girl shut up

Tiana: laughs girl I'm going to bring it with me, so we can read it after school.

Ok we both say before hanging up.

Later that day we meet up to start reading the book together and say wow people really do this kind of stuff?! As we read more and more Mya feels herself getting hot and bothered. The day is fading away so meet me tomorrow with the book because my mama going to be gone, so we will just skip school say's Mya.

Tiana hides the books in her knap sack and heads home! Later after her mom goes to sleep Tiana sneak out the window with the book. Once outside in the shed she begins to read and get to chapter four: Where's My G-Spot! The lights are dim, and the music is softly playing. Keisha kisses on Shondra as Miguel and Jamie is taking turns eating both women vagina, says Tiana as she Continued to read when suddenly two guys she knows appear out of the dark. Brian (short, stocky, Mexican, 5'5, 210lbs) and Drew (Cuban, tall, thin, black hair, 6'0, 250 lbs.)!

POETRY OF
LIFE:PART
ONE

LAKYSHIA L HUBERT
MARY L SHELTON

Poetry Of Life
Part Two

Lakyshia L Hubert
Mary L Shelton

POETRY OF LIFE
PART THREE

Lakyshia Shelton
Lorenzo Shelton Jr
Mary L Shelton
Ray Charles Burnett
Archie Burnett Jr

A CHILDREN'S BOOK TO LEARN, COLOR, PLAY & SEARCH!

Mrs. Lakyshia L Hubert

Let's Help Each Other
*Can You Relate To
These Stories*

LAKYSHIA L.
HUBERT

Toya   Trisha   Monica

My Baby Daddy & The
Family Drama That
Came Along With It!

Lakyshia L. Hubert

SEX IN THE AIR

Let's Get Buck Wild

Lakyshia L. Shelton

Made in the USA
Columbia, SC
27 February 2024